Covid Claus
is Coming to Town

M.J. Edwards

For you, the reader

I'm sorry if you received this as a Christmas present

The person who gave it to you mustn't like you very much

ALSO BY M.J. EDWARDS

Kissing the Coronavirus

Kissing the Coronavirus 2: The Second Wave

Kissing the Coronavirus 3: The Mutant Strain

Kissing the Coronavirus Chronicles: The Complete Collection

Penetrated by the President's Twitter Feed

I F*cking Hate Zoom Quizzes

Campbell's Curse: The South Pier Slayer

The Perfect Poo: A Fiery Fecal Romance

You better not cough

You best not be shy

You better mask up

I'm telling you why…

Dr Holly Mistletoe wanted one thing, and one thing alone this Christmas: a bloody good orgasm. It had been so long since Dr Mistletoe had felt the electrifying effects of a clit-ticklingly enjoyable cumming session. In fact, she struggled to even remember when her last one had been, which was just depressing because she had a really good memory.

It was Christmas Eve and Dr Mistletoe was only just getting round to putting up her Christmas decorations, on account of her being super busy at her job at the zoo as a Zoologist. She'd spent the day doing important zoology tasks, like stroking the zebras, laughing at the penguins (they look so fucking stupid lol) and feeding the cheetahs their pre-Christmas meal of turkey and baked ham.

Dr Mistletoe loved her job, she just didn't love the unsociable hours that came with it. She saw plenty of people during the day, but she'd rarely be able to spend time alone with any of them. No, it was the animals she spent most of her alone time with. And it wasn't like she could do anything sexual with them. Not again.

Her busy zoology hours, mixed with the latest wave of Coronavirus that was sweeping the globe meant social distancing was still keeping the vast majority of willies six feet away from her, and she had a hunger between her legs that couldn't be satisfied.

At that moment, Dr Mistletoe would've killed for a bit of penis.

And by *bit* of penis, she'd have actually preferred a lot. Either size or quantity, she wasn't fussy. Despite having had several penises throughout the course of the year (a record low, she might add), Dr Mistletoe was yet to have a feeling erupt inside of her reminiscent of two freight trains colliding inside a narrow tunnel (the tunnel in this instance being her vagina). She thought back into the deepest, darkest, horniest parts of her mind, desperate to revisit her last orgasm, yet returned with nothing.

She'd come close - a pun she was proud to think of (but was alone so couldn't share with anyone).

A few weeks ago, she'd sucked off the mailman when he put his penis through her letterbox instead of her post. No orgasm.

A month or two back, her old school headmaster had played with her enormous bosom like he was a bongo player and her boobs were the bongos. No orgasm.

During the summer she'd jerked off her sister's ex-husband's accountant and he yelled 'oh superb!' as he ejaculated on her hand. No orgasm.

She'd even thrummed the battered sausage (the name he gave to his penis) of Chippy Stu, the man who worked at the local fish and chip shop. She'd been rewarded with a free bag of chips and, ironically, a battered sausage, but no orgasm.

Dr Mistletoe sighed a big long sigh. Not the sort of sigh that followed really nice coitus, but a frustrated, fed-up sigh, like when you drop a glove in a puddle.

And that metaphorical glove was the only thing that was getting wet this Christmas.

Dr Mistletoe turned on the TV. She needed a distraction to distract her from her horrendously foul, orgasm-less mood.

'And in other news,' said the TV which she turned on, 'Coronavirus cases continue to spiral, putting a dampener on festivities. If things continue as they are, the only thing some kids will be getting in their stockings this year is a positive test result. I'm Dan Daniels, with

Channel 45632072 News.'

Dr Mistletoe swore and turned the TV off again. She hated TV these days because there were always good-looking people on there having orgasms, which made her jealous. Orgasms here, orgasms there, orgasms everywhichwhere.

Except in Dr Mistletoe's vagina, of course.

This whole virus nonsense was ridiculous. For almost two years it had run rife around the world, killing at will. It was like a sinister version of Santa Claus, visiting people when they thought they were safe and giving them gifts. Except the gifts weren't socks and bed and breakfast vouchers, they were coughing fits and hospital stays.

And worst of all, it had severely impeded Dr Mistletoe's ability to experience a vulva invigoration.

Now that the year was approaching its end, she was simply going to have to come to terms with the fact that this year would be the first year since she'd reached sexual enlightenment when she wouldn't partake in the orgasmic sensation of an orgasm.

Unless…

Dr Mistletoe was almost done decorating her tree. She'd wrapped it in baubles and hung the tinsel, and doused it in lights which were as pretty as can be. It looked great - all apart from the absent tree-topper which was yet to top the tree on account of it still being in her hand.

It was a cheeky little porcelain Santa Claus, with bright red cheeks and a twinkle in his eye. He had a pointy hat and presents around his feet, and a welcoming smile that said 'Hey, Dr Mistletoe, heyyyyy…'

It felt so naughty.

But zoology and Coronavirus had taken so many things away from Dr Mistletoe that maybe the naughtiness of it was exactly what she needed to explode with cum.

She rested the lucky little St Nick between her

ample bosom, the little guy disappearing into the valley that was cleavage that went on for days.

She rounded the happy Santa around her boob and made him kiss her pinky browny areola, followed by the centre part of the nipple. It made her giggle like an excitable leprechaun.

Then, Santa made his way down south, and not exactly to the South Pole.

Dr Mistletoe prodded her clitoris with Santa's bulbous nose.

It felt nice. Rather nice, yes.

A grin formed on her mouth.

She teased her gawping opening with his nostrils, then plopped it inside. Hmm, no good. That wouldn't do.

Instead, Dr Mistletoe rammed Santa's hat so deep inside her she began to whistle to the tune of Jingle Bells.

Ooh. Ooh. Oooooooh!

She was close. Dr Mistletoe hadn't felt feelings like

this since the time she'd had sex with a man dressed in just a hat.

She pushed Santa deeper until he was inside her up to his feet. Just the gifts stuck out, and they would hopefully momentarily provide her with a gift of her own.

In and out Santa went.

In.

Out.

Ho ho ho, she thought. She certainly felt like a ho ho ho, with what she was making that poor porcelain Santa do to her.

Something inside her was building.

A feeling of excitement. Of joy. Of release. Of… of…

And then she… she… she…

Sneezed.

Oh.

For shits sake, she thought. How cruel can life be??

All Dr Mistletoe wanted for Christmas was an

orgasm, yet there she was being given nothing but rampant disappointment!

She hurled the soggy porcelain Santa Claus across the room, and it shattered into a million pieces upon the stone hearth.

Coursing through Dr Mistletoe's veins wasn't merriment and Christmas cheer, but anger and animosity and sadness.

It turned out there would be no Christmas miracle after all. Porcelain Santa had been her last attempt at a jizzfest. But alas, she would be left without climax, much like the ending of *The Lord of the Rings: Fellowship of the Ring*. If Dr Mistletoe had to wait another two years to get a satisfying conclusion, much like with Peter Jackson's famous fantasy epic based on the books by J.R.R. Tolkein, she would possibly go insane.

Absolutely nothing was going her way.

She couldn't see her family on account of the stupid

Covid-19.

She had to wait until the last minute to put up her Christmas decorations because her zoology work was all-consuming.

She couldn't even wank herself off to a satisfying conclusion.

Instead, Dr Mistletoe drank away her feelings and watched YouTube videos about Minecraft until way into the night. As she slowly drunkened, tears slipped from her eyes and she sang songs about being sad to herself.

At midnight, her grandfather clock chimed twelve times and was the only company she had to bring in the festive night.

'Curse, you, Santa Claus,' she whispered to anyone and no one. 'I ask for one thing, and yet you cannot deliver it. I hate you, Santa Claus. I hate you.'

Then, Dr Mistletoe left out a plate of milk and cookies (and a carrot for Rudolph, which she knew he'd like because of her background in zoology) just in case Santa showed up. And if he did, she'd be ready to give him a piece of her mind.

Because fuck Santa Claus.

Fuck him good.

Much to her titillation just a few hours later, Dr Mistletoe would get the chance to do exactly that.

***

Dr Mistletoe awoke with a shock at two-thirty-eight and eleven seconds. From above her was a clatter, which sounded suspiciously like several coconuts being banged together on the roof. The strange thing was, Dr Mistletoe didn't remember putting any coconuts on the roof at all.

She sat up and rubbed her eyes viciously, which wobbled her magnificent boobies. She slept in a sexy nightgown, which highlighted just how marvellous her chest plumps were. She caught sight of herself in her mirror, and despite being concerned about the noise on the roof, still took a moment to admire her knockers. She often got compliments about her titties from men, women, zoo visitors, and family members alike. They all said her knockers were the best they'd ever seen, which simply added to her sexual frustrations. She may have been the beholder of two stupendous jubbilies, but because there was nobody around to fuck them, she had to make do with simply tweaking her nips all by herself. She gave her nippy a little toot then hopped out of bed, her Bristols juddering one final time.

Dr Mistletoe took a sip of water from beside her bed. She felt groggy and tired, like she had done the time she'd had sex with the whole of the Manchester United team at the same time. That was a fun Tuesday. But this time she had no crispy dried cum to wash out of her pubic hairs.

Suddenly, awakening Dr Mistletoe from her daydreams about ejaculation fluids, came a thump. Then a clump. Then a drump.

But this time, the sound came not from her roof.

But from downstairs.

Inside the house!

But how could this be? She was home alone, as she had so painfully reminded herself just a few hours before.

There was another bump. Then another. And another.

Then finally, another.

If Dr Mistletoe wasn't mistaken, the sound was… footsteps.

First a clambering sound on the roof, now footsteps inside her home?

It had to be burglars, right?

Because what else could it be?

Because it couldn't be… no… it couldn't be…

Santa? Could it?

No. Of course not.

Or could it?

Dr Mistletoe stood and tiptoed over to her bedroom door, her mammoth tits only bouncing ever so slightly this time. She opened the door so softly, so softly, and listened to the sound coming from downstairs.

'Ho...ho...ugh...'

What the hell was *ho ho ugh*? Santa didn't say *ho ho ugh*. He said ho ho ho!

The stupid burglar in her living room couldn't even get the whole rouse right!

There was a thud and a crash. Then a deep and animalistic groan, like a rhino had just stepped on a cat.

What was that? thought Dr Mistletoe inside her own head.

She stepped out of her room and crept to the top of the stairs. There she could just about see into her living room, where there was a portly shadow slinking back and forth.

'Ho ho ugh,' said the intruder.

And then, Dr Mistletoe heard something that made her aghast. Not another ho, not another thud or footstep or bang.

It was the sound of *chewing*.

Dr Mistletoe couldn't believe her ears! How dare this illegal intruder eat the cookies she'd left out for Santa! What a monster; he must be stopped!

Dr Mistletoe pulled her gun, which she always kept close in event of such a night, out from between her heaving flesh pillows. Her face contracted into one of anger and she leapt down the stairs, gun outstretched.

'FREEZE, INTRUDER!' she echoed.

'Ho ho oh no!' said the hardened criminal.

Dr Mistletoe gasped.

She stared in shock.

She gasped again.

The intruder, it was… was… was…

No.

No, it couldn't be.

No.

But, it was.

It was… Santa.

He had bright red cheeks, redder than the time her bum cheeks had been smashed by the open palm of Big-Hand John, a man she'd had sex with behind the scout hut who had big hands. He had a big, wobbly belly, which was somehow even bigger than her enormous boob region. His beard was wispy and white, like a cloud. His bulbous nose twitched, and the first thing she thought of was how the porcelain Santa had nuzzled against her clit…

'I'm sorry,' said Santa, 'I just needed a few moments to catch my breath. It's been a long and difficult night tonight.'

'Who are you?' asked Dr Mistletoe.

Santa raised his hands. 'Why… I'm Santa Claus of course,' he said, followed by a ten- or fifteen-minute coughing fit.

'But, why are you here?'

'Everyone needs presents at Christmas, Dr Mistletoe,' he said. 'Even overworked zoologists.'

Dr Mistletoe smiled, but that quickly turned to concernedness as Santa began to cough and splutter and make sickening sicky sounds, all while sitting in Dr Mistletoe's chair with half a chewed cookie in his gloved hand.

'What's wrong, Santa Claus?' asked Dr Mistletoe. She wasn't fazed about meeting Santa in the slightest, on account of her having met other celebrities in the past.

'My dear,' he said, spluttering, 'I'm afraid my journey around the globe this evening has taken its toll on me.'

'What do you mean?' she asked.

'This evening I've visited thousands of countries. Many, many towns and cities. More homes than I can count. Unfortunately, for many around the world, the Coronavirus pandemic is still very much a prevalent threat.'

Dr Mistletoe shook her head, jiggling her boobies. 'No...'

'Yes,' wheezed Santa.

'You mean...'

'Yes,' he said, 'I have the Coronavirus.'

Dr Mistletoe stepped forward, extending her hand, 'Let me just—'

'No,' barked Santa. 'You mustn't. I may be vaccinated, and was first in the world to get my booster, but I've been exposed to every strain of Coronavirus on Earth in just a few hours. The disease is inside me... doing things to me no mere mortal could withstand.'

Santa writhed around, hissing and spitting and moaning. Dr Mistletoe watched.

'What can I do?' she asked.

'Nothing, my dear,' he said. 'The magic within me is battling to defeat the virus. But alas, I fear I am losing.'

'What does this mean?' she asked. She glanced down at Santa's groin, which was… was it growing?

She couldn't look away…

'It means,' said Santa, 'that the virus will soon consume my magic.'

'And then what?'

'And then…' he breathed quietly, his voice barely escaping his funky beard, 'I will be able to grant you your Christmas wish.'

'What do you mean?' she asked, searching her brain. Her mind was bubbling with excitement and fear. What had she wished for? She didn't ask for anything, like a soap dish or book on tape; the only thing that she wanted was—

Oh.

Suddenly, she remembered.

She'd asked Santa for…

At that moment, there was a smash. A crash. A bash. A flash.

Santa began to change.

His enormous jelly belly sucked in.

His man boobs tightened and became firm, like those of a muscular kangaroo.

His skin morphed from snow-blushed pink to a mushy pea shade of green.

His arms and his legs turned and toned in like they were made of wagyu beef.

His chin became visible below his beard, like it had been chiselled from pure bronze.

And his penis. Oh, his penis.

It was glorious.

It was as if the lord had designed it himself, like a gigantic marrow that had recently won first prize in a marrow growing competition at a local church's family fun day.

He was no longer Santa Claus, friend to children the world over.

He was a sexy hunk beast, with a willy that made her toes curl at just the sight of it.

When Santa finally stopped contorting and transforming, Dr Mistletoe was able to continue breathing, her beating heart making her tits thrash all over the place.

'Santa Claus?' she asked, her voice naught but a squeak.

'I am no longer Santa Claus,' he said, his voice deeper than that big BWAH sound from the *Inception* trailer.

'Then who are you?' she asked, her knickers moistening at the sound of his pure manliness.

'I am,' he said, then paused dramatically, 'Covid Claus.'

'Oh my,' said Dr Mistletoe.

'I have a present for you,' he said, standing so tall his red hat brushed against the ceiling.

'Oh?' asked Dr Mistletoe, even though she knew what that present was, she was just being flirtatious because she wanted him to outright say it.

'Yes,' he nodded. 'I'm going to make you cum like you've never cum before.'

'YES DADDY COVID CLAUS,' screamed Dr Mistletoe and she ripped away all her clothes to reveal her naked body to him, which was super hot and lovely and she of course had the big tits and her bum and her legs were really nice too.

They dove at one another, their lips locking and their tongues disappearing down each other's throats like their stomachs were magnets and their tongues were hot metal.

Then, Covid Claus battered her breasts, kneading them like he was a baker and her tits were freshly proven dough. He began masticating her nipples, his thick lips flumping against her areola, the bumps on the skin surely spelling out 'holy shit that feels good' if they were to be read like braille.

Dr Mistletoe fumbled for Covid Claus' cucumber cock, which she bent down and forced so far into her mouth that she could taste every single bite of the milk and cookies he'd eaten that night. She made slopping noises, like a horse licking peanut butter off wet jelly. Covid Claus hummed and grunted and very low and deeply said —

'Ho ho ho.'

'Oh yes,' said Dr Mistletoe with a mouthful of penis.

Then, Covid Claus pulled her up by her breasts,

and flipped her over the sofa so she was on her knees. Using his serpent-like tongue, Covid Claus began lapping at her vagina, while his bulbous nose nestled against her bum hole. Once or twice, as his tongue stretched extra far inside her canyon of wonders, his nose said a cheeky little hello to the inside of her bottom.

Dr Mistletoe had never felt anything like it before. She gushed fluid and it oozed out onto Covid Claus' willy, like her body was commanding him to enter her vaginally with his incredible appendage.

'Now it's time for me to show you what's really inside Santa's sack,' said Covid Claus. He twisted Dr Mistletoe over onto her back, and her legs instinctively shot skyward like two proud flagpoles. Meanwhile there was a third, even prouder flagpole between her legs, which crammed into her open vagina hole like a train entering the Channel Tunnel.

Covid Claus thrust like he was trying to start a fire

inside Dr Mistletoe's vagina.

It was so hot which was ironic considering it was Christmas, which is generally quite cold unless you're in Australia which is usually rather hot. Hot like the sex she was having.

Covid Claus grappled with Dr Mistletoe's norks, slapping them about like they were a delicious joint of pre-roasted Christmas ham. He gnawed on them like they were, too.

And then, with a final, agonisingly deep thrust of his jolly green groin, Santa sneezed his jingle sperm all over her labia while she simultaneously had an orgasm that sent her through time and space itself. She temporarily exited the astral plane as her whole body felt like she'd become the manifestation of that little prickle you get when you get a static shock.

She burst.

She burst good. All over.

'HOLY GOD,' she screamed over and over.

Covid Claus took off his hat and wiped their combined juiciness away from his softening member, like it was a balloon with the air slowly being let out of it.

Then, Covid Claus tossed his hat to Dr Mistletoe, and said, 'Something to remember me by.'

'Don't you worry,' she said, climbing down from the sofa and stretching her legs to release more of Covid Claus' spunk from her vaginal vestibule. Her knees were weak, and she wasn't sure whether or not she might collapse at any moment. 'I'm going to remember this for the rest of my life; I don't think I've ever felt anything quite as magical—'

Dr Mistletoe looked up, but Covid Claus was gone.

But… that was impossible.

He'd been there one moment, but now it was like he'd never been there at all.

But he must have been. Her pussy was still echoing

with the call of pleasure his mammoth member had given her.

Had she dreamed it?

Had her encounter with Christmas' sexiest anti-hero been all in her head, and the pool of moisture on the floor simply a result of a faulty washing machine?

No.

It couldn't have been.

Dr Mistletoe made a tsk sound and cleaned up the gloop from the floor. The whole time she had a really sad look on her face, like she'd been told she'd won the lottery only to have it taken away from her a few moments later.

The lottery in this scenario being Covid Claus' dick.

Still, whether her orgasm had been real or not, it had felt real. And that was what mattered the most. She'd go to bed, wake up and have Christmas dinner then go to work and do zoology things, because even at Christmas the zoo animals still had to be cared for. Even if her pussy hadn't been.

Dr Mistletoe trudged up the stairs.

Perhaps Christmas miracles didn't happen after all.

But then, as Dr Mistletoe reached her bedroom and moped inside, she saw something resting delicately, and soggily, on her pillow.

It was Covid Claus' hat.

Then a smile burst onto her face, just as her orgasm had burst out of her fanny.

Maybe it had been real all along.

ABOUT THE AUTHOR

MJ Edwards is a writer and wicket keeper in her local cricket team. She had previously promised that *Kissing the Coronavirus 3: The Mutant Strain* would be her last Covid book, but she took inspiration for Covid Claus after reading an article and learning about how Santa Claus travelled around the world and went into millions of homes. She's buying her ferrets a new chew toy for Christmas, so they stop biting the sofa cushions.

She is dating a nice man called Malcolm who treats her nice and gave her a new scarf <3